Morris
The Millionaire Mouse

Written by Melanie Martin
Illustrated by G. Brian Karas

Troll Associates

Library of Congress Cataloging-in-Publication Data

Martin, Melanie.
   Morris, the millionaire mouse.

   (Fiddlesticks)
   Summary: Overjoyed when he wins the million-dollar
raffle, Morris Mouse decides to quit his job and buy
everything he's ever wanted.
   [1. Mice—Fiction.   2. Wealth—Fiction.   3. Conduct
of life—Fiction]   I. Karas, G. Brian, ill.   II. Title.
III. Series.
PZ7.M36412Mo   1989   [E]   88-1235
ISBN 0-8167-1339-1 (lib. bdg.)
ISBN 0-8167-1340-5 (pbk.)

Morris was a hard-working mouse. He worked in Mr. O'Hare's grocery store. Morris mopped floors. He stacked cans into tall piles. He carried out heavy bundles of groceries for shoppers. The work was hard, but Morris didn't mind. He liked his job.

Payday came once a week. Morris didn't make a lot of money. He had to be careful how he spent it.

But every week Morris set aside one dollar for something special. That special thing was a million-dollar raffle ticket.

"I'll take one raffle ticket, please," Morris told Mr. O'Hare. Morris gave Mr. O'Hare a dollar. Mr. O'Hare gave Morris a raffle ticket. Every week it was the same thing.

Morris really didn't expect to win the raffle. But there was always a slim chance that one dollar would earn him a million. It was fun to imagine that!

On the day of the raffle, Mr. O'Hare always turned on the radio so everyone could hear the winning number.

"Today's million-dollar-raffle winner is . . ." said the announcer, "number 82187!"

Suddenly, there was a loud crash! A mountain of cans hit the floor and bounced here and there. *Plink! Tink! Klank!* Cans rolled everywhere.

"What happened?" cried Mr. O'Hare, running down the aisle. "Morris, are you all right?"

PLink!
Tink!
KLank!

. . . Number 82187!

Morris was sprawled on the fallen cans. There was a stunned look on his face. In his hand was a raffle ticket.

"I—I won," said Morris.

"What?" asked Mr. O'Hare.

"I—I'm a millionaire," stammered the mouse.

Mr. O'Hare squinted at his friend. "A millionaire," he grunted. "Morris, did you fall on your head?"

Morris staggered to his feet. "The winning ticket," he explained. "I have it. The winning number is 82187! That's my number!" He handed his ticket to Mr. O'Hare.

Mr. O'Hare studied the number on the ticket. "You're right," he exclaimed. "You won. You really are a millionaire! Congratulations!"

A short time later Morris claimed his prize. Customers crowded around as Morris showed the check to Mr. O'Hare.

"What are you going to do with all that money?" Mr. O'Hare asked.

Morris scratched his head. "I don't know," he said.

"I know what I'd do," said Chip Monkey. Chip didn't like to work. He liked to hang around with his friends, Sam Sloth, Pearl Pelican, and Harvey Hippo.

Morris looked at Chip. "What would you do?" he asked.

Chip smiled. "I'd never work again," he said. "I'd buy lots of things. And I'd have a party every night."

Morris thought about Chip's answer. Working was hard. He didn't need money anymore. He had a lot of it. So why work?

"I'm not going to work anymore," Morris said. He looked at Mr. O'Hare.

Mr. O'Hare smiled and nodded. "I'll miss you, Morris. But I understand."

"I'm going to spend my money," shouted Morris, as his eyes twinkled strangely. "I'm going to buy things I've always wanted. I'm going to buy things I never had."

He glanced at Chip. "And I'm going to have a big party to celebrate. Everyone is invited."

Morris Mouse did not skimp on his party. He rented a big hall and hired a band to play music. And food? Morris bought out the store. Tables were filled with everything from hot fish cakes to cold strawberry shortcake. There were barrels of pickled green bananas, platters filled with ten-pounder hamburgers, and mounds of chocolate-covered peanuts.

"The food is great," Sam Sloth told Morris.

"It's super," said Harvey Hippo.

"And it's free," Pearl Pelican whispered to Chip Monkey.

"Morris, you shouldn't have spent so much money," said Mr. O'Hare when the party was over. "You should be careful how you spend." Mr. O'Hare was starting to worry about Morris.

"I'm a millionaire," said Morris. "I don't have to be careful. I don't have to work." He pointed at the mess left by the party. "I don't even have to clean up. I hired someone else to do it."

The next day, Morris visited Mr. O'Hare. "Come with me," Morris said. "I want to show you something." The mouse led Mr. O'Hare to the top of a steep hill. Parked on the hill was a shiny new car.

"Is this your car?" asked Mr. O'Hare.

"It's mine," answered Morris proudly. "It cost a lot, but it's worth it. This car is special. Get in. I'll show you why."

Mr. O'Hare climbed in the car. "What's so special about it?"

Morris got behind the wheel. "I'll never have to spend a penny on gas," said Morris. "This car doesn't use gas." He released the brake.

Zip! Down the hill the car sped. It
reached the bottom and rolled a bit.
Then it came to a stop.

"What's wrong?" asked Mr. O'Hare.

Morris shrugged. "I don't know. The car
looked good when I bought it."

"We'd better check the engine," said
Mr. O'Hare. He got out and opened the hood.

"Now I know why you'll never have to spend a penny on gas," said Mr. O'Hare.

"Why?" asked Morris.

"This car has no engine," replied Mr. O'Hare. "Didn't you look under the hood before you bought it?"

Morris shook his head.

"I guess we'll have to push it back up the hill," said Mr. O'Hare.

"Oh no," cried Morris. "That's too much like work. And I'm never going to work again. Leave the car here. I'm rich. I'll just buy a new one." Then he quickly added, "One with an engine, this time."

Mr. O'Hare put his hand on his friend's shoulder. "Morris, you must try to spend your money wisely. If you don't, even a million dollars won't last very long."

Morris nodded. "I need the help of someone who knows how to handle money," the wealthy mouse admitted. "Will you help me?"

"Yes," said Mr. O'Hare.

"Good," said Morris. "Let's go to my house and talk this over."

Mr. O'Hare walked Morris home. "You have a nice little house," said Mr. O'Hare to Morris.

Morris stroked his chin thoughtfully. "It is little, isn't it?" he remarked.

That strange twinkle was in the mouse's eyes again. "A millionaire shouldn't live in a little house," Morris said. "I'm going to buy a big new house—a giant house." Away he ran before Mr. O'Hare could stop him.

Morris bought the biggest house he could find. It cost a lot, but Morris didn't care. "How do you like it?" Morris asked, as he showed Mr. O'Hare around.

Mr. O'Hare didn't like the house. "It's too big," he answered. "Walking from one end to the other could tire you out."

Morris stopped in his mouse tracks. "Walking is like work," said Morris. "I'll have to take care of this."

Mr. O'Hare smiled. He was sure Morris would sell the great big house.

The next day Morris invited Mr. O'Hare back to his new house. "I solved the walking problem," said Morris.

"Let me guess," said Mr. O'Hare. "You sold the house?"

"Nope," answered Morris. "Wait here. You'll see what I did." Morris went into a room.

VA-ROOM! A loud noise echoed through the big empty house. VA-ROOM! VA-ROOM! Out into the hall rode Morris on a brand-new motorcycle.

"No more walking," said Morris. "From now on we ride from room to room. Hop on."

Mr. O'Hare couldn't believe his eyes.
"Morris," he cried, "a motorcycle isn't the
answer. This house is too big for you. All the
rooms are empty. No one lives in them."

Morris thought a minute. "I agree," he
said. "What's the sense of having a big house
with a lot of empty rooms? I'll invite people
to live here with me."

Who went to live with Morris? Soon anyone who was lazy and didn't want to work moved in. Before long, Chip Monkey, Pearl Pelican, Sam Sloth, and Harvey Hippo were right at home in the big, roomy house.

"Morris," said Mr. O'Hare, "this won't last long. Pretty soon you'll get tired of this."

Mr. O'Hare was right. Before long, Morris was tired of doing nothing all day.

"This is boring," said Morris, as he and his house guests sat around the pool. "I don't want to work, but I don't like being idle. Even a millionaire should do something." He looked at Chip. "What do millionaires do, anyway?"

Chip scratched his head and nudged Harvey. Harvey glanced at Sam Sloth.

"Well?" said Morris.

"Millionaires need to relax," said Sam Sloth.

"That's right," agreed Chip. "You need to relax, Morris."

"Relax?" muttered the mouse. "How?"

"Fishing," said Pearl Pelican. "Fishing is relaxing."

Morris smiled and nodded. "Okay. I'll try it," he said.

Morris bought a huge fishing boat. He bought rods, reels, and all sorts of fancy fishing lures. Then Morris and his friends went out to fish.

But fishing wasn't much fun. The fish
wouldn't bite. Morris started to get angry. "I
spent a lot of money to relax," he grumbled.
"And I haven't caught a single fish. I want
to relax. I want to catch some fish."

Chip grinned at Morris. "It's only
money," the monkey said. He took out a
dollar bill and tossed it into the water.
"What's money to a rich mouse like you?"

Suddenly, a big fish leaped out of the
water and snapped up the dollar bill.

"That's the problem," cried Sam Sloth.
"We're using the wrong kind of bait. These
fish are money-hungry."

Morris took out his wallet. "Everyone grab some bait," he said. "I have plenty."

The rest of the day Morris and his friends fished, using money for bait. They caught a lot of fish. And they spent a lot of money doing it.

However, fishing wasn't fun or relaxing for too many days. Morris soon got tired of it. So he gave up fishing. He bought a garage to store the boat and the fishing gear in.

"You've got to stop spending so much money," Mr. O'Hare told Morris, as they sat around the house.

"Stop worrying," answered Morris. "I have a lot of money. I'm more worried about what to do all day. I don't like doing nothing."

Chip Monkey wanted to keep Morris happy. He knew that even millionaires have to work at times. But he didn't want Morris to know that. So he made up a story. "When millionaires don't relax," said Chip, "they play. That's what you should do."

"Play?" said Morris.

"That's right," agreed Harvey. "What do you like to play, Morris?"

Morris thought a minute. "Baseball," he answered. "I like to play baseball."

"Well, buy a baseball stadium, and let's play ball!" shouted Pearl. Sam Sloth nodded.

Mr. O'Hare leaped to his feet. "Don't do it, Morris!" he said. "We can play baseball in the park, and it won't cost anything."

But Morris had that strange look again. "Don't worry," he said to Mr. O'Hare. "I have a lot of money. If I'm not going to work or relax, I have to play. I'll buy a stadium."

A baseball stadium wasn't all Morris bought. He bought silk uniforms and expensive baseball gloves, too. He even hired a famous baseball team to play against his team. Boy, did that ever cost a lot of money!

On the day of the game there was one thing missing. "There are no fans in the stands," Chip said to Morris. "The game will be more fun if a crowd is watching."

That strange twinkle flickered in the mouse's eyes. "Chip is right," he said. "I'll give a dollar to anyone who will come to the game."

Soon the stadium was filled with excited
fans. Every one of them was a dollar richer,
thanks to Morris. They cheered loudly when
the game started. It didn't take long for the
cheering to stop. The contest was one of the
worst baseball games in history. The famous
team was very good. And Morris Mouse's
team was very bad. The fans in the stands
got up and started to leave.

"Where are they going?" groaned Morris. "How can I make the fans stay?"

"Buy everyone a hot dog and popcorn," Chip suggested. "They'll have to stay to eat the food."

Mr. O'Hare glared at Chip. "Do you know how much that will cost?" he grumbled.

"It doesn't matter," said Morris. "Feed the fans. I want them to stay."

	1	2	3	4	5	6	7	8	9	
WORLD CHAMPION TEAM	5	5	5	5	5	5	5	5	10	50
MORRIS' TEAM	O	O	O	O	O	O	O	O	O	Ⓞ

Mr. O'Hare bought hot dogs and popcorn for everyone in the stadium.

The fans stayed to eat. They certainly didn't stay to enjoy the game. Morris Mouse's team lost, 50-0.

The day after the game, Mr. O'Hare went to see Morris. He had some bad news.

"Morris, I got the bills for yesterday's game," he said. "In order to pay them, you'll have to sell everything you own—the house, the boat, the motorcycle, the car, everything."

"Everything?" said Chip Monkey.

"Everything?" said Harvey Hippo.

Sadly, Mr. O'Hare nodded. "Yes, everything," he said. "Morris is no longer a millionaire. He's no longer rich. Morris Mouse is flat broke."

Chip Monkey fell off his chair. Harvey Hippo gagged on a sandwich.

"Gee," said Sam Sloth. "I thought a million dollars would last forever."

"It didn't," said Mr. O'Hare.

Chip and his friends started to walk away. "The vacation is over," Chip said. "Call us if you ever become a millionaire again, Morris."

Morris watched as all of his guests packed
and left. Soon he and Mr. O'Hare were all
alone.

"Do you know, I think they only liked me
because I was rich," said Morris.

Mr. O'Hare nodded. "It's true," he said.
"Try not to feel too bad, Morris."

Morris smiled. "I don't feel bad at all,"
he replied. "I feel good. I'm glad they're
leaving. I'm glad I'm broke. Being rich really
didn't make me happy. I was happier before,
doing a job that I liked." He looked at
Mr. O'Hare. "Can I have my old job back?"

"Of course!" said Mr. O'Hare. "You can
start tomorrow."

The next morning, Morris reported for work. He had fun stacking up tin cans. He enjoyed mopping floors. He even liked carrying out heavy bags of groceries. It felt good to work again. He didn't miss being a millionaire one bit.

At the end of the day Morris went up to
Mr. O'Hare.

"I made a mistake," said Mr. O'Hare. "I
looked over the figures. You're not flat
broke."

"I'm not?" asked Morris.

"Nope," said Mr. O'Hare. "After selling
everything and paying all the bills, you have
one dollar left." And he handed the bill to
Morris.

Morris took the money. "I know just what I'm going to do with this dollar," he said.

"What?" asked Mr. O'Hare.

"I'm going to spend it on something special," said the mouse.

Morris handed the dollar bill to Mr.
O'Hare. "I would like one raffle ticket,
please," he said. He looked at Mr. O'Hare
and grinned from ear to ear.

Mr. O'Hare gulped and handed Morris a
ticket. "Suppose you win again?" he asked.

Once more, that strange twinkle appeared in the mouse's eyes. It flickered, and then it faded away.

"If I ever win a million dollars again," said Morris, "I'll spend it wisely, and I won't quit my job. Now I know I'm happiest when I'm working hard!"

And that's the story of Morris the millionaire mouse.